OF SHADOWS

Karen Dolby

Illustrated by

Adrienne Kern

Series Editor: Gaby Waters

Contents

Reader Beware . . .

This is a chilling ghost story – but there's more to it than meets the eye. The mystery will unravel as the story unfolds, but if you keep your eyes open you may be able to solve it yourself.

Vital information could be lurking anywhere. On almost every double page there are things that could help you. The pictures are important, so look at them carefully. And make sure you read the old documents thoroughly. But don't be fooled. There may be some false clues . . .

Page 48 will give you some hints of what to look out for. You can refer to this page as you go along or look at it at the end to see if you missed anything.

The Telegram

Ned and Kit Light were packing when the mysterious envelope arrived. Tomorrow they were moving to another house in another town, a long way away. Kit spotted the strange foreign stamp at once, then she read the words 'For the urgent attention of the Light Family' and ripped it open.

URGENT TELEGRAM

AN IMPORTANT MATTER CONCERNING A LOST ANCESTOR AND A SURPRISE INHERITANCE HAS COME TO LIGHT IN MYTHIKA. YOUR ASSISTANCE IS URGENTLY REQUIRED. PLEASE TRAVEL TO MYTHIKA AT ONCE FOR FURTHER DETAILS. PLANE TICKETS ENCLOSED FOR MR. AND MRS. TOM LIGHT. SPEED ESSENTIAL.

FROM MARCUS DALLY, LAWYER, ON BEHALF OF DEPARTMENT OF LOOSE ENDS, MYTHIKA.

The Day of the Move

The Shiftitkwik Removals' van screeched to a halt outside Number 1, Spectral Lane, an old house standing all alone at the end of a long, narrow road on the outskirts of a small town called Hallows-on-the-Hill. The Light family followed close behind in their car and found Mr. Grey, the leasing agent, waiting impatiently outside the front gates.

Ned and Bullseye, the dog, peered up at their new home. Dark, diamond-shaped windows stared back at them. Weeds sprouted in the drive and tall iron gates leaned crazily against the crumbling walls. A decaying sign, half hidden by weeds still hung from one gate. "Hallows Grange, to Rent" it said. Meanwhile, Mr. Light signed the grubby documents that Mr. Grey flung at him and Mrs. Light checked the road map for their route to the airport.

Kit stared open-mouthed as their belongings whizzed past and disappeared into the dark interior of the house. Promising to send the bill, the removals' men waved and disappeared in a cloud of exhaust fumes. Mr. Grey sped away in the opposite direction.

Ned and Kit were left feeling slightly dazed as they said goodbye to their parents and tried hard to sound cheerful. Both thought about their parents' mysterious mission. What would they find in Mythika? Who was their lost ancestor . . . and what was the surprise inheritance?

They waved until the car was out of sight and then turned to the house. Suddenly, as if from nowhere, a short, very old man appeared. Smiling, he walked up to them.

"So, you're moving in . . . into the house of shadows," he said, pointing to the house. He paused, then added so softly they could hardly hear, "You might be the ones . . . they've been waiting."

"What do you mean?" Kit asked, "Don't go . . ." but the man turned away, vanishing into a thick mist which suddenly swirled around them. Kit glanced at Ned, who shrugged and tapped his head.

"Nuts," he said. "Come on, let's go inside."

Hallows Grange

Inside, the house was damp and chilly. Kit shivered in spite of the warm day outside. "The house of shadows," she muttered, staring out of the window. "The name suits it."

"Look what I've found," Ned grinned, after rummaging through one of the boxes. "Food! This will cheer us up."

Crunching chocolate chip cookies, they began to explore. They drew back curtains and threw open the windows, but the house remained gloomy and cold. Ned looked wistfully out at the sunny garden.

The old house was strangely silent and their footsteps echoed as they walked through rooms filled with odd, old fashioned furniture. Kit stared at the pictures on the walls, wondering who had lived here before, when a clock began to chime. Ned and Kit both jumped at the sound and it was then that they heard a faint tick tock, tick tock, growing slowly but surely louder and faster.

"It's as if the house is slowly coming back to life," said Ned, thoughtfully.

Kit wanted the attic room as her bedroom. She liked the sloping, beamed ceiling and the comfy brass bed. She lugged her bulging suitcase up the narrow, rickety staircase, but as she reached the top, flickering shadows skipped across the ceiling.

The little room was icily cold. Kit shivered. Then a sudden noise made her turn and she froze, rooted to the spot, as a radio lying on the bed crackled to life. Kit knew that she hadn't switched it on.

Suddenly, the attic didn't seem such a good idea. Bumping her suitcase behind her, she scooted downstairs, almost tripping over Bullseye who was growling at . . . at nothing.

Kit bent down and patted the dog. She glanced up just in time to see a fleeting shadow which for an instant looked like a young girl. But that was impossible. She shrugged and laughed nervously, "First I hear things, now I'm seeing things. This old house is giving me the creeps."

Soon, all was forgotten as Kit and Ned munched their way through a huge supper of beans, toast and chocolate, in front of a roaring fire. But Ned had the uncomfortable feeling he was being watched and Bullseye prowled the room sniffing uneasily. Suddenly the lights dimmed, then flared brightly, the curtains billowed and an owl hooted. At the edges of the room the shadows gathered and a thin white mist filled the air.

A Strange Scene

Kit and Ned stared unbelievingly as the swirling mist grew so dense they could hardly see. The air was filled with a strange, choking smell, like smoke and their heads spun dizzily. Then, as swiftly as the mist had come, it disappeared and the air was clear.

Kit looked around in confusion. They were sitting in a different room. Or were they? The furniture was new, bright sunlight shone through an open window and an unknown dog lay on the rug in front of them. But there was something very familiar about the layout of the room . . .

Ned ran to the window. "This is incredible," he said, as he began to climb out. Kit looked out in amazement, then followed him.

"It's like a film set," Kit croaked, when she finally found her voice. She paused. "Or as if we've been transported back in time."

No one took any notice of Ned or Kit, or even seemed to see them. Kit jumped out of the way as a small boy chasing a pig headed straight for her. She had the weird idea that he would simply have run on through her, as if she wasn't there. It was almost as though they were invisible.

"Look at the house!" cried Ned, turning suddenly. "It's grown." They gazed back in disbelief. Their house was recognizable, but it formed just a small side wing of a larger, more impressive stone building. What had happened? Kit was struggling to make sense of it all when the huge oak doors of the big house were flung open.

A tall, sinister figure, in a long flowing coat stepped out and stood framed by the doorway. Was it Ned's imagination or did everyone pause and shrink back? Kit and Ned looked on in silence as a scene unfolded in front of their eyes, like an act from a play. As they watched, the players seemed to move in slow motion as if the scene was often rehearsed and repeated. Kit had a strange feeling that she had heard the words before.

A young girl pleaded with the man in the long flowing coat. "Please Mr. Hubble, don't take my brother away."

Mr. Hubble ignored the girl and marched briskly to a waiting carriage. He was followed by a pale faced boy who looked about the same age as Ned. Mr. Hubble waited impatiently, looking at no one, while the boy's mother and sister said a tearful goodbye, then he grasped the boy roughly by the arm and pulled him inside.

From the window of the carriage, Mr. Hubble stared back at the house. His piercing eyes looked straight through the spot where Ned and Kit were standing. Kit shivered as the man smiled, not warmly, but with a cold, evil grimace. The carriage rumbled away along the cobbled track and the boy's mother stood crying, whispering to herself, "I know I shall never see him again . . ."

As Ned and Kit looked on, a chilling mist appeared as if from nowhere, shrouding the house and swallowing everyone around it. Their heads began to spin and the scene faded . . .

Night Falls

They were back where they had started, sitting in front of the roaring fire. Ned and Kit turned to one another. What was going on? What had they witnessed – a scene from the past? Was it possible? Suddenly Kit yawned, all she wanted was to go to sleep. Ned felt tired too, so tired that he could hardly keep his eyes open. It was late and perhaps things would make more sense tomorrow. The house could wait till the morning . . . But the house, or something in it, had other ideas.

Ned opened his bedroom door. He shivered. Something strange was going on. What was that peculiar feeling? It was almost as if . . . as if he was waiting for something to happen. Trying hard to ignore it, he climbed into his new bed. He tossed and he turned but it was no good. He was wide awake now. Perhaps it was because of the moonlight streaming into the room through the uncurtained windows. Perhaps . . .

Suddenly Ned sat upright in bed and as if obeying a secret voice, he stared at the ornate mirror standing on the chest of drawers opposite. At first the mirror was a gleaming blank. It reflected nothing. Then, with a shock, Ned saw a different room in the glass. Lit by sunlight, it was still his room, but furnished as it would have been years, maybe centuries before.

He gasped as he saw a face reflected in the glass. It was like his own, but not his. It was the face of the boy they had seen earlier with the sinister Mr. Hubble. He looked pale and ghostly and stared at Ned as if he could see him . . . as if he wanted his help. Then the boy turned to the door and Ned heard the faint sound of someone crying.

Meanwhile, Kit was sleeping peacefully with Bullseye lying happily across her feet. Her new bed felt warm and snug and she had quickly forgotten the strange experiences of the day. Instead she was dreaming of imaginary adventures in sunny Mythika, of her parents on their mysterious mission, of a surprise inheritance and an endless supply of enormous strawberry ice cream sundaes that were almost too big to eat . . .

Her dream didn't last long, however, and Kit reluctantly returned to Hallows Grange. She woke with a start to the sound of angry voices.

Kit blinked in the darkness, feeling sleepy and confused. She stared in disbelief at two ghostly figures who were arguing angrily at the foot of her bed.

"Never!" the girl's voice screamed.

Moonlight flooded the room and Kit saw the girl's face clearly for the first time – she was the sister of the pale faced boy in the strange scene from the past.

The ghosts, or whatever they were, seemed to become more solid and real in front of her eyes as her own room grew fainter.

"I'll never agree!" the girl shouted, racing from the room, closely followed by Mr. Hubble.

They seemed to run straight through the wall, but when Kit looked again, she saw the outline of a door emerging and growing solid. Kit could make no sense of what was happening, but she knew she should follow the girl. She slipped out of bed and tiptoed to the door that had just appeared in the wall. Slowly she turned the handle.

House of Shadows

The door opened and Kit stepped out of the room. She gasped in amazement. An apparently endless corridor stretched in front of her, lined with the sort of pictures and furniture she had only seen in museums. She was in a different house . . . or was she? Then she remembered the strange scene they had witnessed earlier and the answer became clear. Long ago their home had once been part of a much bigger house and she was now inside it.

A shiver ran down her spine. Was it fear or excitement? Kit couldn't tell. She began to walk, almost as though she were dreaming and would wake at any moment, yet she had the curious feeling she was being led somewhere, or was looking for something.

She stopped with a jolt. As she stared into a gold-edged mirror, she saw . . . nothing! There was a hazy glow, but she had no reflection. She stepped back and sideways and shook her head, but still saw only the wall behind her. What was happening?

"I'm a ghost here," she whispered, shuddering. Suddenly, all she wanted to do was go back to bed and wake up in her own home in her own time, but something made her go on.

Candles burned brightly in their holders along the corridor. The flickering light sent shadows playing across the ceiling and walls. She marched bravely on and, turning a corner, saw a heavy red curtain moving. Had someone brushed against it recently? Kit looked again and realized that it was drawn across the entrance to another passage. She slipped through and shivered as an icy blast of air whistled around her. The curtain billowed out behind her.

"I don't want to walk along here," she thought.

Was it her imagination, or did someone really hiss in reply, "You must. Hurry!"

Kit began to walk quickly, faster and faster until she was running. As she ran, Kit became aware of someone crying. Where was the sound coming from? Ahead or behind? It seemed to be everywhere.

Kit ran up and down stairs, opened doors and stared into deserted rooms. As each door opened, she hoped to reach the end of her search. On and on she raced, but still the crying continued. She was sure it was Catherine, the girl she had seen in her room.

The crying was as loud as ever, leading Kit further into the old house, yet she never seemed to get any closer. She saw no one but in each room she felt certain that someone had left only seconds before.

Breathless and confused, she finally stopped. In the shadows of a conservatory, half hidden by tropical plants, stood the grim figure of . . . Mr. Hubble. Slowly, he turned around. Kit gulped. Everything went black.

A Spooky Message

Ned yawned and stretched. "I had the weirdest dream," he muttered to Bullseye, who had just slunk into the room.

He blinked and opened his eyes wide in surprise as he caught sight of the mirror opposite and read the thin, spidery letters written across the glass.

Meanwhile, Kit stirred in her sleep. Her bed felt strangely hard and lumpy. Awake, but with her eyes still shut, she realized she felt very cold, and something prickly was tickling her nose.

She opened one eye suspiciously. This was definitely NOT her bedroom. Where was she? She sat up quickly and found herself fighting her way through a huge and very spiky yucca plant.

"What am I doing here?" she spluttered, looking around at the ruins of the crumbling conservatory. She had been lying on an old stone bench.

The last thing she remembered was Mr. Hubble's sinister stare. Kit shivered at the thought of it.

"Ned won't believe this . . ." she muttered to herself, walking slowly back upstairs. Kit hardly believed what had happened herself.

Ten minutes later, Ned and Kit finished their stories. "We can't both just have been dreaming," said Kit, staring at the writing on Ned's mirror. "There's something very strange about this house. No wonder that old man called it the house of shadows."

Bullseye growled. Kit grabbed Ned's arm. "Look," she whispered, pointing through the open door. Ned stared and from the expression on his face, Kit knew he could also see . . .

A ghost! In the doorway stood a pale shadow of a young boy. As they watched, he turned to face them staring into their eyes with a sad, helpless expression. Neither was surprised to recognize the boy who had disappeared in the carriage with Mr. Hubble, the face Ned had seen reflected in the mirror.

"Don't go," Kit called hesitantly, but the shadowy figure began to fade, growing almost transparent before he vanished into the air.

Later, slurping hot chocolate and munching toast in the sunny garden, Ned and Kit tried to make sense of things. "I know we've been seeing ghosts," said Kit at last. "But I get the feeling it's the house that's haunting us, showing us snippets of what happened here in the past . . . something awful."

"But why?" asked Ned, not expecting an answer. "If only we knew more, like what happened to the big old house and who lived here. But how can we find out?"

Ned and Kit stared at one another and exclaimed together. "That weird old man!" He definitely seemed to know more than he said yesterday. And it was he who had first mentioned the house of shadows. He was their only lead. If they could find him, maybe he could explain.

Hallows-on-the-Hill

Ned looked at Kit. "Well?" he asked. "Come on. What are we waiting for? Let's go into the town and find him."

But Kit had already gone. Ned raced after her, struggling into his jacket as he ran. Bullseye frolicked around his feet, happy to be outside. Behind them the house watched, guarding its secret.

Hallows-on-the-Hill, as well as being farther away than it had looked, was also much bigger. In despair, Kit gazed around her at the bustling streets and shops. "Where do we start?" she asked, glumly.

Ned shrugged, then turned decisively down one of the busiest looking streets. Occasionally, someone looked at them curiously as if wondering who they were, but most people hurried by, intent on their own business. Kit began to wonder what they had hoped to find out here. There were certainly no clues leaping out at them.

"We'll have to find someone to ask about the house and the old man," she said, finally. A small grocery store seemed a good starting point.

Ned quickly chose a bar of Mango Melts and casually tried to question the shopkeeper. "Um . . . we've just moved into Hallows Grange and wondered if . . ." he stopped.

There was a shocked gasp. As if by magic, the crowded shop emptied. The shopkeeper shoved Ned's change at him and said abruptly, "We're closed." With that, Ned and Kit found themselves back outside.

Even more determined, they decided to try somewhere else. They chose a bustling cafe with a friendly looking owner and waitress. Perched on stools at the bar, Ned and Kit began again. This time, Ned decided not to say where they lived. He described the old man they had seen, aware of a prickly silence around the cafe. Then several people began talking at the same time.

Neither the cafe owner nor the waitress would say more. Kit and Ned were left feeling more confused than ever. They walked slowly on, heading for the old town walls in gloomy silence. It was very still and quiet when they heard a familiar voice.

"Ned, Kit – I believe you were looking for me," it said.

A Sorry Tale

Ned and Kit spun around to see . . . the old man. Ned felt cold shivers run down his spine as the man greeted them. How did he know their names? "Creepy!" he thought to himself. One look at Kit told him she felt like running away, too. But they had to stay. They wanted to find out about the house of shadows and Ned was more certain than ever that the man knew something.

"You've seen the house of shadows," the man said. "I knew you would."

Kit nodded. "How did you know?" she asked. "What do you mean?"

"My name is Amos Goodfellow and I shall tell you what I can," the old man replied. "Hallows Grange has been haunted for as long as anyone can remember. People have seen flickering shadows, heard whispered voices and felt icy hands touch their faces. Some have even seen the ghostly outline of the house of shadows – the big house from the past."

He paused and looked at them for a moment before continuing his strange story, a tale so vivid that Kit and Ned could almost picture the scenes in their mind.

The house has been empty for a long time. People say it's too damp or too dark, but everyone knows those aren't the real reasons.
Long ago the house and all the land nearby was owned by the Golightly family.
They were fair and respected landowners and the house was famous for its parties and hospitality.
Then disaster struck and the house changed hands under sinister circumstances. Mr. Hubble, the new squire, was cruel and miserly. Both he and the house seemed cursed and when half the house was destroyed by fire, there was no money left to rebuild.

Soon only the west wing remained – where you live now. The rest simply tumbled down out of neglect.

To
Rent

A Shadowy Figure

Kit turned to ask another question, but Amos had vanished as mysteriously as the first time they had seen him. "It all seems a bit far-fetched to me," she said. "And I don't know how much I trust that man. His disappearing trick is too convenient – he tells us just enough to keep us interested."

Kit and Ned scuffed their way home. They had learned something about the house, but most of their questions were unanswered.

As they walked through the gates of Hallows Grange, Kit stared hard at their house. A curtain moved and then twitched again. A shadowy figure darted out of sight. Someone, or something was in there. Kit suddenly felt very angry. "I'm sick of these tricks . . . If it's someone's idea of a joke, it isn't very funny. I want to know exactly what IS going on!" she yelled at Ned, who watched in amazement as Kit stormed up to the house. She flung open the front door and ran inside.

Ned arrived to find Kit in the kitchen, red in the face with embarrassment, and speechless. A friendly woman in an apron seemed to be emptying boxes and . . . he sniffed, cooking something delicious. Ned was still trying to decide precisely what was in the saucepan and wondering whether it could be for them, when he realized that he hadn't a clue who this woman was.

"I'm Tilda Daly," she said, before Ned asked. "Your parents asked me to help out while they're away."

After his third bowl of soup, followed by a mega helping of rhubarb crumble swimming in custard, Ned began to feel very comfortable and at home. He listened sleepily as Kit, now over her embarrassment, chatted to Tilda. He guessed she was trying to find out more about Hallows Grange.

"There have always been stories, of course," Tilda said. "Because it's an old house, people claim to have seen . . . things, you know. But you don't want to listen to that nonsense. I've never seen anything."

"Do you know anything about the history of the house and the people who used to live here?" Kit prompted.

"Hallows Grange has been empty for a long time now," Tilda said. "If you want to know anything about it, there's a whole stack of books and even some old photos and things which were left here. They're in a trunk in the attic, I seem to remember. And there are always the portraits – mind you, they're a funny-looking bunch."

Kit felt like kicking herself. Of course they should have looked at the portraits and she had even glanced at the trunk in the attic. The house itself was the obvious place to look for information. She was sure that the answer to all their questions was here and an eerie voice inside her head told her that the house itself wanted them to discover its secret.

In the Attic

There was a large trunk in the attic, bound with bands of metal and heavy brass clasps. Surprisingly, the chest was not locked. The lid creaked open to reveal a curious and amazing assortment of books, clothes, pictures and other mementoes. It looked as though it had not been disturbed for centuries. Kit delved in and began sorting through.

June 13th 1791

HMS MEDUSA SINKS NO SURVIVORS

The criminal transportation ship, The Medusa, has been lost off the coast of Mythika in heavy seas. Her captain, Carruthers Crook, has sailed the ship safely through these waters for more than 10 years. Captain Crook and his crew were lost with the ship. There were no survivors.

LAWRENCE'S ...NGERS

...E STARTS NOW!

...boned corsets

April 10th 1790

Jebediah Grimshaw

Are your instructions clear? I don't want to know the details, but Thomas must be separated from the others. There must be no doubt . . . I will pay you five guineas at the harbour when The Endeavour sails. The 30 guineas will be yours when you return . . . alone. The choice of crew is up to you.

Ebenezer Hubble

The clock chimed the half hour, then the hour . . . and a second hour. The shadows lengthened, but Ned and Kit were too busy to notice. At first they just glanced at the old letters, notes and papers, feeling more than a little guilty, as if they were snooping. But curiosity and the overwhelming sense that they were meant to be there soon took over.

Shadows Gather

Kit sighed as she finished reading. She felt that she still knew very little. The eerie voice in her head seemed to tell her it was all connected with Thomas Golightly's will and the sinister Mr. Hubble. She shivered. Was this why she and Ned were being haunted? Someone wanted their help – could it be to foil some dastardly plan plotted by the evil Hubble?

Kit noticed for the first time how dark the room was. Out of the corners of her eyes she could see the shadows gathering. She and Ned sat unable to move. The mist thickened and seemed to swirl around them. Their heads reeled as the room spun and they knew, even before the dense mist cleared, that they were now in another time . . . in shadow time.

They watched transfixed as a scene unfolded before their eyes. Just as before, when they first saw the house of shadows, it was as if they were watching an act from a play. But as the story emerged, they realized that the scenes were being played in reverse order.

The light faded, leaving Ned and Kit in the darkness, waiting for something they both knew would happen without knowing what it might be. The moon rose to reveal a study. The door slowly opened and Edward slipped silently into the room, unaware of the sinister figure lurking half hidden in the shadows behind a chair.

The figures disappeared. Kit and Ned now found themselves outside among some trees, blinking in the sunlight. Edward and Catherine were talking in hushed voices.

Kit had heard enough. She already knew what would happen. She ran to where Edward was standing. "Don't do it," she yelled. "It's a trap."

Ghosts from the Future

Kit grabbed Edward's arm and pleaded once more, "Don't take the money. It's a trap."

She knew it was useless. She had no way of making Catherine and Edward hear. Yet they seemed to sense something.

"How strange," said Edward, brushing her unseen hand away, "I felt an icy hand touch my arm."

"And did you hear something?" asked Catherine in an anxious voice. "Words I couldn't catch, a ghostly whispering."

The edges of the trees grew faint and blurred as the scene faded. Mist swirled and their heads spun. Once again Ned and Kit returned to their own time and the twilight of the attic.

"Edward could feel it when you touched him," Ned exclaimed. "It was as if you were the ghost."

"We WERE the ghosts," Kit replied slowly. "Ghosts from the future, being shown a glimpse of the past . . . It's as if a story is being told to us."

"But not in the right order," Ned added.

"I've just realized something," said Kit, almost whispering with fear. "Catherine and Edward . . . those are OUR real names."

"It could be a coincidence," Ned began. But he knew it was more than that. Some secret voice told him their own fate was somehow tied up with this brother and sister from so long ago. The idea made Ned feel cold and threatened. But part of him knew it was true.

"Let's go," said Ned, closing the trunk. "Nothing else is going to happen today."

As if in answer, the light flickered, growing suddenly bright and then dim. Ned and Kit blinked in the gloom as mist engulfed them. They were in the study again. Once more the door creaked open. This time, they watched Hubble creeping stealthily into the room with a sheet of parchment in his hand. He looked furtively around, took out a small gold key from his pocket, and then opened one of the desk drawers.

"What is he doing?" Kit whispered.

It was so dark it was hard to see much, but Hubble seemed to be looking for something. He paused and then pulled out a paper edged with a green border. He smiled as he tucked it swiftly inside his coat and carefully replaced it with the red edged parchment he had been carrying.

The room and Hubble grew pale and transparent. A thin mist filled the air and a familiar dizziness brought them swiftly back to the attic. Suddenly a small window blew open and a gust of wind howled around the room, lifting an ancient, faded newspaper from a wooden casket in the far corner. The wind died as suddenly as it had come, dropping the yellowing newspaper open at their feet. They began to read.

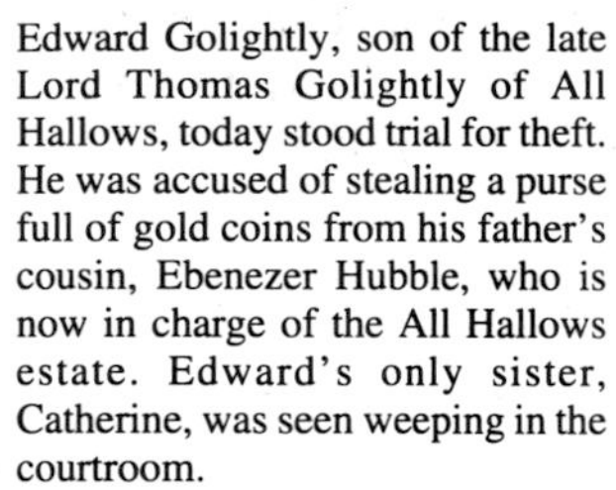

The Daily Crucible

LORD'S SON FOUND GUILTY OF THEFT FRIDAY February 24th, 1790

Edward Golightly, son of the late Lord Thomas Golightly of All Hallows, today stood trial for theft. He was accused of stealing a purse full of gold coins from his father's cousin, Ebenezer Hubble, who is now in charge of the All Hallows estate. Edward's only sister, Catherine, was seen weeping in the courtroom.

Ebenezer Hubble is himself a judge, not noted for softness - he won last year's Judge Jefferies award for sending more prisoners to the gallows than any other judge. At yesterday's trial he was quoted as saying, "It saddens me to bring the boy to trial - he is my beloved cousin's son. But he had disgraced the family's reputation and shamed his father's name. Justice must be done, however painful."

Judge Hubert Stern, a former pupil of Mr Hubble's summed up by saying, "The overwhelming evidence against the boy leaves me no alternative but to sentence him to seven years' transportation to the colonies."

Many were shocked by the harshness of the punishment. Edward Golightly will sail on The Medusa, which leaves on March 30th.

Artist's drawing of Edward Golightly in the dock.

Fashionable headresses at

NOTHING NATURAL

The Golightly family announces the sad death of Lady Constanza Golightly from influenza on February 22nd. Relative, Ebenezer Hubble, would not comment upon whether stress due to the sad case of her son, Edward, had hastened her untimely demise.

MONSTER SPOTTED OFF MYTHIKAN COAST

An incredible prehistoric sea monster has been spotted near the Mythikan coast. Reports have been pouring in. Some claim the ferocious monster is as big as a galleon, others say it is the size of a large whale. Eye witness, Able Seaman John Silver claims he saw the monster swallow a small fishing boat including the crew and nets.

Tomorrow will be published
THE NEW JEST BOOK
Jests, witticisms and famous sayings of
DR SAMUEL JOHNSON
At all good booksellers now.

Looking for a cure for pimples, eruptions, red noses? Look no further than **DR QUACK'S AMAZING TONIC**.

Tomorrow will be published by P. Usborne of Saffron Hill, a **WHOLE LENGTH PORTRAIT** in mezzotint of **REAR ADMIRAL C. POOPDECKER**, Bart, Fellow of the Royal Society.

Just published
THE WHIM OF THE DAY, for 1791.

Tonight, at the Royal Hall, Drury Lane, the renowned, chocolate-eating child musical prodigy, Foxgang Musteat, will give his first piano recital in London.

Ned and Kit finished reading. They now knew the sad fates of both Edward and Mrs. Golightly.

"The Medusa!" Kit exclaimed, remembering the newspaper clipping they had found in the trunk. "That was the ship that sank," she sighed, feeling strangely stunned and surprised. "Poor Edward must have drowned."

As she spoke she glanced at the open wooden chest in the corner of the room, where the newspaper had come from. At the bottom lay a yellowed, but familiar-looking sheet of paper. Kit was amazed to find another will by Thomas Golightly, but this was different from the one they had already seen.

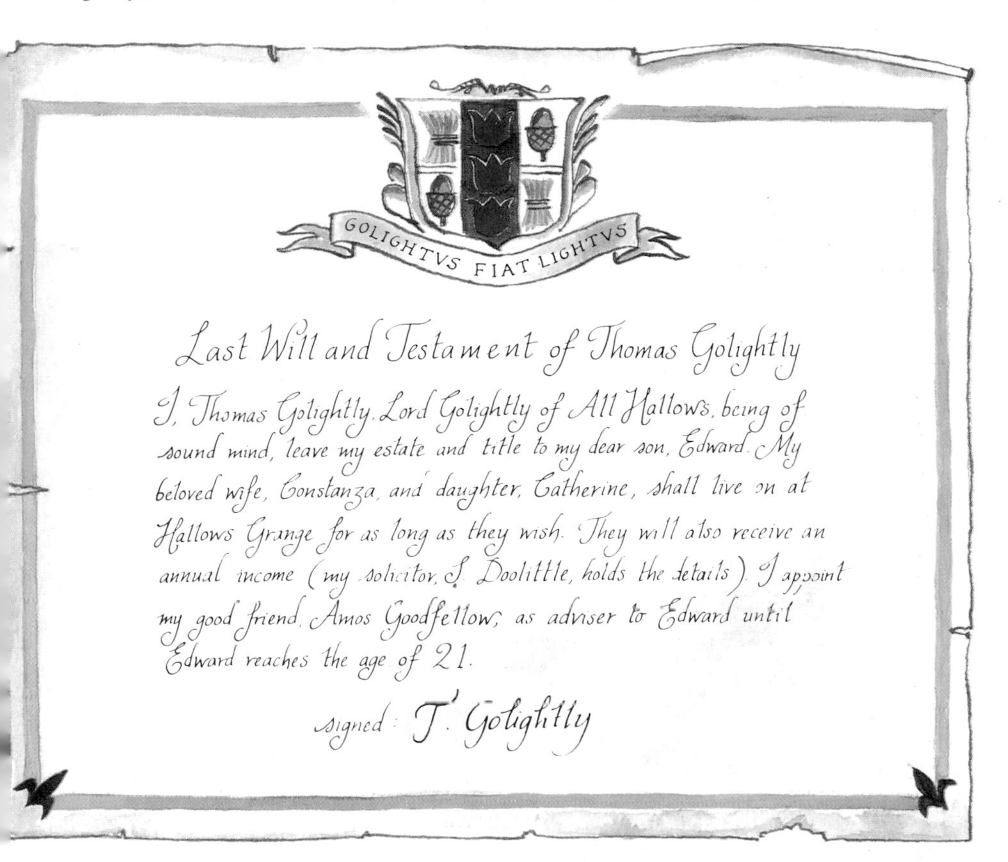

GOLIGHTVS FIAT LIGHTVS

Last Will and Testament of Thomas Golightly

I, Thomas Golightly, Lord Golightly of All Hallows, being of sound mind, leave my estate and title to my dear son, Edward. My beloved wife, Constanza, and daughter, Catherine, shall live on at Hallows Grange for as long as they wish. They will also receive an annual income (my solicitor, J. Doolittle, holds the details). I appoint my good friend, Amos Goodfellow, as adviser to Edward until Edward reaches the age of 21.

signed: T. Golightly

Kit was puzzled. What did the two wills mean? She replaced the will and newspaper in the casket and closed the lid. Absent mindedly, she wiped away the thick layer of dust to reveal a shiny mahogany top. To her horror, she found herself gazing down at Ebenezer Hubble. He smiled his sinister smile. Kit's gasp broke the spell. As Ned, too, stared down, the image vanished.

The Story Unfolds

Kit and Ned walked back down the rickety attic stairs. "Things seem to be speeding up," said Kit.

"Perhaps we're building up to the climax of the final act," Ned said.

"I wonder why Thomas Golightly changed his will," Kit pondered. "And WHY did he leave Hubble in charge?"

"But DID he change his will?" asked Ned. "Hubble was switching papers in the study and the one he took away looked suspiciously like the will we've just seen. Suppose the other one leaving him in control is a forgery? I wonder what happened to Thomas Golightly?

As if in answer, the shadows grew solid and characters materialized, coming to life as yet another scene unfolded before Ned and Kit's eyes. A group of people stood gathered in a library. Kit recognized the familiar faces of Edward and Catherine, their mother and Mr. Hubble. The rest were strangers, but who was the old man – the spitting image of Amos Goodfellow?

Everyone looked very solemn as the man sitting at the desk placed a pair of spectacles carefully on his nose. He cleared his throat and began to read out the will of Thomas Golightly. As he did so, Kit knew with a peculiar certainty that this scene and the last were being shown in the correct order. But why? Could it be that whatever power was responsible for revealing these snatches of the past, was determined that the truth of Hubble's actions should not be lost or mistaken.

A shocked gasp ran around the room. Amos started with surprise and looked alarmed while the others whispered anxiously together. Only Hubble looked unsurprised and smirked to himself.

The scene faded and changed. Kit and Ned were now looking at a group of familiar figures in the room. Suddenly Kit realized that the past was rewinding once more and this unhappy episode came before the reading of the will.

The temperature dropped suddenly. Kit and Ned found themselves sitting on the steps of a bustling dockside. A ship was being loaded ready to sail. Edward, Catherine and Mrs. Golightly stood with a man Ned guessed was Thomas Golightly. Meanwhile, Hubble whispered furtively with a man they had never seen before. He seemed to be handing over a purse full of money.

Hubble's Diary

Kit and Ned were still shivering from the cold and damp when they felt the now familar spinning sensation. They found themselves back inside the house of shadows, alone . . . with the sinister Mr. Hubble.

"This is getting confusing," hissed Ned.

"There's no need to whisper, he can't . . ." Kit stopped.

Hubble spun around and stared blankly in their direction. He looked puzzled.

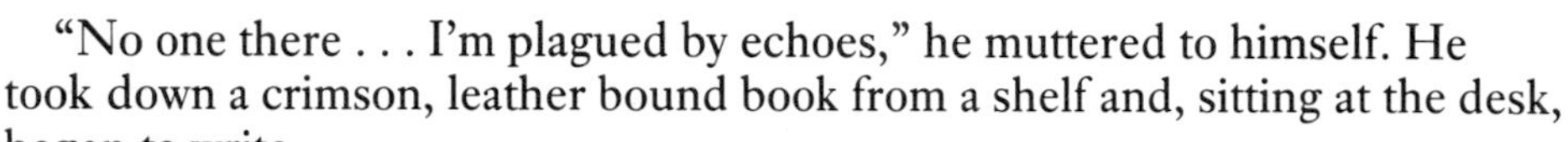

"No one there . . . I'm plagued by echoes," he muttered to himself. He took down a crimson, leather bound book from a shelf and, sitting at the desk, began to write.

Curiosity got the better of Kit. Stepping silently forward, she peered over Hubble's shoulder and quickly beckoned Ned. "It's his diary!" she almost exclaimed, remembering to whisper just in time.

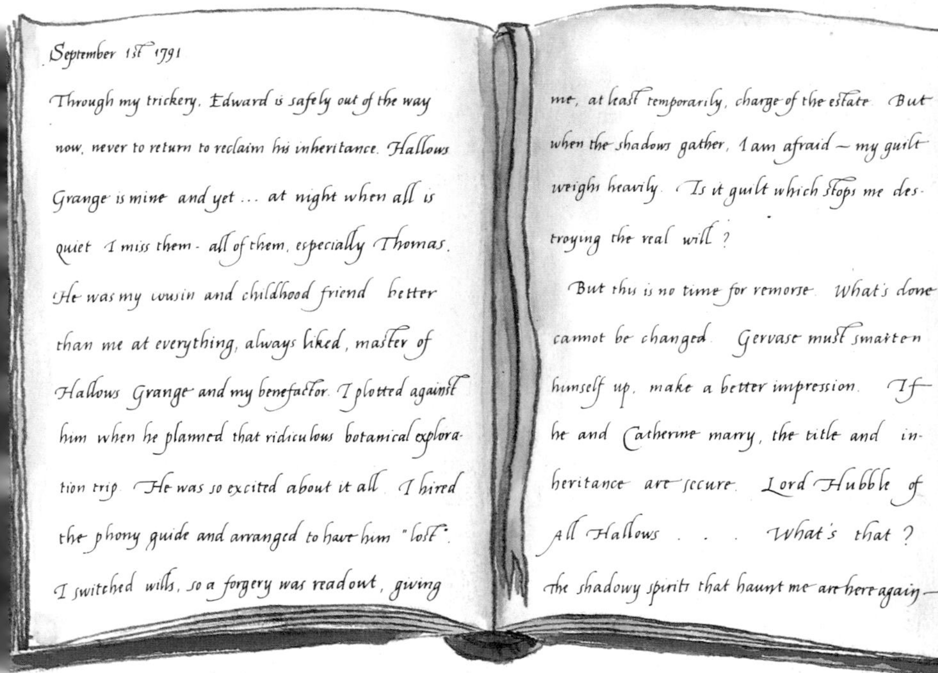

September 1st 1791

Through my trickery, Edward is safely out of the way now, never to return to reclaim his inheritance. Hallows Grange is mine and yet ... at night when all is quiet I miss them - all of them, especially Thomas. He was my cousin and childhood friend better than me at everything, always liked, master of Hallows Grange and my benefactor. I plotted against him when he planned that ridiculous botanical exploration trip. He was so excited about it all. I hired the phony guide and arranged to have him "lost". I switched wills, so a forgery was read out, giving me, at least temporarily, charge of the estate. But when the shadows gather, I am afraid – my guilt weighs heavily. Is it guilt which stops me destroying the real will?

But this is no time for remorse. What's done cannot be changed. Gervase must smarten himself up, make a better impression. If he and Catherine marry, the title and inheritance are secure. Lord Hubble of All Hallows . . . What's that? The shadowy spirits that haunt me are here again –

Ned and Kit were still reading when Hubble stood up suddenly, sending them flying to avoid him. He began to pace around the room talking aloud. Something told Kit and Ned that time had moved on from the other scenes. Hubble was now master of the house.

Startling News

Both Ned and Kit were asking themselves the same question. Why had the letter shocked Hubble so much? Ned snatched at the paper as it fluttered down, catching it before it reached the floor. Eagerly, he and Kit began to read.

Mythika
August 5th 1791

Dear Madam,

You do not know me, but I was Midshipman on HMS Medusa. I wish you to know that your son, Edward, did not perish with the ship as thought. He is alive, though very weak and being cared for here in Mythika. He seems to have lost his memory and needs his family's help and support.

He and I were the sole survivors and I myself do not expect to survive my injuries. I am dictating this letter to a kindly soul here. I am worried about your son. I came to know him well during the voyage and am convinced of his innocence of any crime. I could not rest easy knowing his plight so far from home.

Your obedient servant,
Samuel Tar

Kit nudged Ned. "He looks as if he's seen a ghost."

That was exactly what Hubble thought he was seeing, or not seeing. He stared in horror at the letter which looked as if it was floating in mid-air.

"I'm doomed!" he wailed. "I hear voices whispering in my ear and now spirits, sent to haunt me forever." He paused and then in a different, crafty tone spoke aloud to the room. "This changes nothing. My plans will succeed and Edward can rot in Mythika. No one will ever know he is alive."

With that, he stormed from the room. Everything blurred and grew misty. When Kit and Ned could see again they were back in their own time. Kit slumped into the nearest armchair. It was hard to keep up with events. The more they found out about Ebenezer Hubble, the more evil he seemed.

"But why are we being shown all this?" puzzled Ned feeling exhausted. "What are we supposed to do?"

"I think we'll know when the time comes," Kit replied.

The door creaked open. Kit and Ned stared expectantly, but it was only Bullseye. He sniffed the air suspiciously, growling as the fur rose on his neck. All at once the television flickered to life and three figures appeared on the screen – Hubble, his son Gervase and Amos!

"They're talking about Catherine," exclaimed Ned, as the picture faded. "She must have drowned after poor Edward was sent away."

Kit jumped at the sudden noise as the telephone rang. It was their mother speaking from a long distance, but it was a bad line and the phone went dead before she had finished. Kit stared wondering at the receiver. "The name . . . the Golightlys must be our ancestors," she gasped at last. "We HAVE to save Catherine and tell her Edward didn't drown. NOW I'm certain our lives are linked to theirs." A silent voice seemed to whisper that this was their mission.

A Stormy Night

Poised for action, Ned and Kit stood waiting. But there were no shadows, no familiar swirling mist. In fact, everything was disappointingly normal.

"I suppose we must wait until the house is ready to show us what happened next," said Ned.

The night passed agonizingly slowly and the next day dragged unbearably. Neither felt they could leave the house for fear of missing something, but it was hard to do anything. They tried listening to music, watching television and playing games. They raided the fridge for endless snacks and even Bullseye was restless. At last Kit said what they had both been avoiding.

"Perhaps the haunting has stopped. We know what happened. Shadow time has moved on – Hubble and the letter, and the television scene must have happened months after Thomas Golightly died and Edward was sent away."

But as evening drew on, the house grew strangely hushed and expectant. Darkness fell and the shadows lengthened. An eerie chill crept through the rooms and voices whispered, always just out of earshot. As the mist swirled and their heads reeled, Ned and Kit knew they were once more ghosts from the future in the house of shadows.

They were alone. All was quiet except for the rhythmic tick tock of the clock. Catherine! They knew they had to find her, now, tonight.

"Come on," exclaimed Ned. "We know that Catherine drowned. We must find the lake."

They dashed outside into storm-lashed darkness. Wind howled through the trees and thunder crashed. Only lightning ripping across the sky made it possible to see anything. But where was the lake? As far as Kit knew, there was no lake in their own time. It seemed hopeless, but Ned struggled on. He felt as if he had been there before and knew instinctively which direction to take. Kit followed, battling blindly through wind and rain, desperately hoping Ned was right.

As Kit stumbled through the lashing rain, she realized that they were not the only ones outside on this wild and windy night.

Hubble and his son spoke in desperate tones as they ran from the house.
I couldn't stop her . . . she means to do it.
Which way did she go?
The stable boy was busy in the yard.
Steady boy. You've a long ride ahead tonight with Miss Catherine.
Amos waited anxiously in the shadows beside a small gate.
I hope Catherine is safe. I should have done more to help her escape. At least the storm should keep Hubble out of the way.
Catherine ran through the trees dressed as a boy, carrying a bundle of clothes.
Of all the bad luck . . . bumping into Gervase.
She headed for the lake . . .
Catherine is escaping. She must be planning to fake her drowning.
But Hubble knows Catherine is up to something. He will try to stop her . . . and we must stop him.

Lakeside Struggle

Ned and Kit hurried on through the trees. They could no longer see either Catherine or Hubble.

"Maybe he's gone the wrong way," yelled Kit, above the noise of the storm. "Perhaps he didn't see Catherine."

Ned was doubtful. "Catherine is in danger. I know it."

Suddenly the lake was in front of them. At first they could see no one. Then Kit gulped in horror. There on a narrow wooden jetty, above the wild, wind tossed water . . .

Was Hubble trying to stop Catherine, or . . .? With a sick feeling in her stomach, Kit knew what would happen next. "She's going to fall and then nothing and no one will be able to save her," she cried. "Come on. We've got to do something!"

But what? They were invisible to the two struggling figures.

"We have to distract Hubble. Remember the letter? He thought he was being haunted," Ned exclaimed, running towards the jetty. "We can use Catherine's cloak."

Kit advanced on Hubble, the cloak billowing in front of her. Ned seized the boat's oar. To Catherine and Hubble it must have looked as if ghostly, unseen hands held the cloak and brandished the oar. Catherine stared in amazement. Hubble looked terrified. He started in horror, backing away from Catherine. Did she realize the "ghosts" were on her side? As Hubble shielded his face, Catherine slipped quickly away through the trees.

Kit flung the cloak over Hubble's head. Ned overturned the boat and threw Catherine's abandoned hat to the waves. To Hubble's eyes, when he finally fought off the cloak, it would look as though Catherine really had drowned.

Graveyard Search

The last thing Kit and Ned saw was Hubble, free at last from the cloak, staring at the upturned boat and bobbing hat. With that, the wind wailed deafeningly. Whirling leaves blurred the scene, then silence. Damp and bedraggled, they were back in their own time.

It was the next morning before Ned and Kit discussed the events of the previous night.

"I still think there is something else," mused Kit. "I don't believe that is the end of the story."

She wandered across to the window and stared out. The figure sitting on one of the broken statues confirmed her feeling. "It's Amos," she yelled, running outside. Ned was close on her heels.

Amos was as elusive as ever. He also seemed to know exactly what had been happening to them.

"I can't stay long," he began. "But you must be prepared. Remember what you have seen and where. Time has passed and Hubble is a haunted man . . . haunted by his own fears, and guilt. His end is near. The date is significant. At the appointed hour, it's up to you."

"What do you mean?" Ned asked. But it was too late. Amos had given his message and as before, in the instant when they glanced away, he had vanished. "Who is he anyway? Is he the Amos we've seen with Catherine and Edward? And how does he know so much?" Ned grumbled.

"Perhaps he's a link between shadow time and our time," Kit muttered. "He said, '. . . his end is near. The date is significant . . .' What date? When did Hubble die?" she paused and then exclaimed, "Maybe the answer is in the graveyard. It's very old. Come on."

The graveyard was quiet and deserted. Enclosed by a moss covered wall, with sheep grazing in the surrounding fields and lit by a bright autumn sun, it was not a bit creepy.

"The oldest graves seem to be over here," said Ned, leading the way. They knew the church was old, but was it old enough? And even if Hubble WAS buried there, his grave might have disappeared long ago.

Sunlight filtered through the trees and there were even some flowers, but the farthest corner was strangely dark and gloomy, as if shrouded in permanent shadow. Kit knew instinctively that was where they should look. Standing a little apart from the rest she found Hubble's gravestone. Was it imagination that made her shiver, or had it grown suddenly colder? Ned pushed aside the long grass and brambles to read the inscription. It was amazingly clear, as if only recently carved.

"Look at the date," he whispered. "It's today."

A Will is Read

Darkness was falling by the time Kit and Ned were home again. Kit blew on her frozen fingers to warm them up. "If the date means anything, something should happen today," she said.

Ned looked dubious. "But what?" he asked. "And what did Amos mean when he said it's up to us?"

It was not long before a familiar mist swirled through the house. The darkness grew blacker and the shadows more dense. With their heads spinning, Ned and Kit found themselves in the house of shadows. Again, a storm raged overhead. Windows rattled and the house shook with each crash of thunder. They were alone in a room. Filled with a sense of urgency that something important was happening, they ventured out into the hall and up the stairs.

A low hum of voices came from Hubble's room. Ned opened the door and they slipped silently inside. No one appeared to notice. Kit gulped at the grisly scene in front of her. In the middle of the room, lit by flickering candlelight, propped high on snowy white pillows lay Ebenezer Hubble. A man they had seen before began reading in a solemn voice.

At the lawyer's words, Gervase pulled out a handkerchief and sniffed noisily. "Stop blubbing, boy," growled Hubble from the bed. For a moment Kit felt almost sorry for Gervase.

A blast of cold air and the sound of the door quietly opening and shutting anounced the arrival of someone else.

It was Amos! His piercing eyes looked directly at Kit and Ned as if he could see them. Ned shuffled uneasily. The buzz of voices began to fade until he was only aware of a strange, unnatural silence.

Something was expected of them. Ned's eyes were drawn to the shelves above the desk. A red book – he knew it was Hubble's diary! It held the evidence of his dastardly crime. Solomon Doolittle of Doolittle and Dally must be made to read it.

To the startled group gathered in the room it looked as if a ghostly hand swept the shelf clear. They ducked the flying books which thudded to the floor. One, a bright red volume, landed open in the hands of a shocked looking Solomon Doolittle. He began to read aloud.

All for Nothing

All eyes turned to stare at a horrified Hubble. He gasped and sat bolt upright. "You win after all," he croaked to the air. He pointed to the desk. "All for nothing," he whispered and sank back on the pillows.

Everyone gazed at the desk, but were too shocked to wonder what Hubble was pointing at. Ned knew. Slowly he lifted the lid of the wooden casket.

Only Amos moved. He took out three pieces of paper. Ned and Kit were not surprised to see a small newspaper clipping, the genuine will of Thomas Golightly and a familiar looking letter.

"I knew the will was hidden somewhere, though I didn't know where. But the letter is an amazing discovery," Amos spoke so quietly that only Kit and Ned could hear.

They expected the scene to fade at any moment and to find themselves back in their own time. But this was not quite the end.

There was a sudden commotion outside in the hall and a knock at the door. A footman announced the arrival of Lady Golightly-Smarte.

"Who?" Ned glanced at Kit, who looked equally puzzled.

The door opened. All eyes turned expectantly and saw . . . Catherine. She walked slowly into the room, followed by a tall young man. She looked uncertainly at the group gathered around Hubble's bedside.

"What is happening?" she asked. Catherine glanced anxiously at Hubble. "I received a mysterious message telling me to come urgently, and that it was now safe to return."

Amos smiled. With that the scene faded. Ned and Kit found themeselves not in their own time, but outside in brilliant, hot sunshine. They saw Catherine walking with Edward, still weak from his illness. Amos and Henry looked on.

The story seemed finally complete. Kit and Ned had discovered the secret of the old house and righted the ancient crime. They looked back at the house of shadows for the last time.

What Happened Next . . .

As the outdoor scene faded, their own time solidified around them. Kit and Ned were back inside the house in their own familiar surroundings. Bullseye wagged his tail, pleased to see them. It was two days later when a letter from their parents thudded down onto the doormat.

Hotel Loukanikis
Mythika

September 14th

Dear Kit and Ned,

Hope you are well and not too bored or lonely. We have lots to tell you.

I don't know why they dragged us all the way to Mythika, it seems to be something of a mystery. I told you about your great grandfather changing the family's name - well, it looked as though we had a rather shady ancestor in the distant past that no one knew anything about. As a result, we had been left a few old Mythikan coins and pots. Then suddenly, today, everything changed. A letter had appeared - no one seems to know where from. Mr. Dally could tell us the whole story.

Our ancestor was called Edward Golightly and he only lived on Mythika for a short time. He had been shipwrecked here. He was ill and had lost his memory. The poor boy was only your age Ned, and he didn't have a clue who he was until his sister and her husband eventually rescued him and nursed him back to health at home. Guess what...you'll never believe it, but his estate was Hallows Grange - that old heap we're renting! I know it's a bit of a wreck at the moment and not very big now, but with a little hard work it will soon feel like home.

We'll be back as soon as we can get a flight.

Lots of love,
Mum

Ned and Kit read and reread the letter. Everything seemed to make sense now, including their own link with the Golightly family. But the house held one more surprise.

A strange, new tingling sensation ran down their necks accompanied by a roaring sound that grew louder and louder until it was almost deafening. The ground seemed to shake as dead leaves and papers flew through the air, caught in a sudden whirlwind. Then there was silence and the air was instantly calm.

"What's happening?" whispered Kit. One cautious look told her they were still in their own time. "The house feels different."

Ned and Kit stared at one another. Together, they raced outside as the same incredible idea occurred to them both.

"The house of shadows," Ned gasped.

"As it always was, as if nothing had gone wrong, and the Golightly family had never left," added Kit. "No one could describe it as a 'bit of a wreck' now. What shall we tell Mum and Dad?"

Did You Spot?

You can use this page to help spot things that could be useful in solving the mystery. First, there are hints and clues you can read as you go along. They will give you some idea of what to look out for. Then there are extra notes to read which will tell you more about what happened afterwards.

Hints and Clues

3 What's in a name?

4–5 What do you think the old man's message could mean? Watch out – you might see him again.

6–7 What spooky portraits! Could this be a case for some serious art appreciation?

8–9 Do you recognize the sinister Mr. Hubble? And what about the face framed by the carriage window?

12–13 Do you notice anything strange about the way Ned and Kit look?

14–15 The message on the mirror reads, "Help". Someone seems to be in trouble, but who?

16–17 The townspeople are behaving very strangely indeed . . .

18–19 What a mine of information Amos is.

20–21 Do you recognize the man in the portrait? Have you noticed the date?

22–23 Read all the documents carefully.

26–27 Kit and Ned are shortened versions of Catherine and Edward. What about their parents' names? The document Hubble is carrying looks familiar . . .

28–29 Try and sort out the useful from the useless here. Did you know that the Latin word "fiat" means "becomes"?

30–31 This man is called Amos and he looks like Amos – could this really be Amos?

32–33 The diary may be important later on.

34–35 Mythika – that's cropped up before. Could there be a connection? Do you recognize Gervase?

38–39 A guilty conscience at work here.

40–41 What could Amos's cryptic message mean?

42–43 Does one of the names Doolittle and Dally ring any bells? Look back right to the beginning of the book.

By the Way...

Who was Amos Goodfellow? Was he from the past or present? Perhaps Kit was right when she described him as "a link between shadow time and our time" – a ghost trying to right an ancient wrong and save his friends the Golightlys from tragedy. After all, Amos mysteriously disappeared once Edward and Catherine were safely home and Hallows Grange was restored to its original size.

Gervase Hubble married Dolores Shrimpton and opened the only kebab restaurant in All Hallows. It was a great success and still exists as the cafe Kit and Ned visited. Gervase, known to his friends as Gerry, had never been happier. He and Dolores had seven children and one of their descendents still runs the cafe today.

Kit in particular was delighted to discover that, along with Hallows Grange, their family had inherited a holiday home in Mythika.

Before Ned's and Kit's involvement in their family history, Edward had continued to live on the island of Mythika, having lost nearly all memory of his previous life. He could only remember his name and the country he came from. Years later, his grandchildren moved away hoping to discover their family's roots. They failed and later changed the family name to Light. After Kit's and Ned's strange adventures in the house of shadows, Edward was quickly pardoned of any crime and returned to his home. He married a girl from Mythika and lived happily in Hallows Grange for the rest of his life.

First published in 1993 by Usborne Publishing Ltd, Usborne House, 83-85 Saffron Hill, London EC1N 8RT, England.

First published in America June 1993

Printed in the UK. Universal Edition